to
Matthew
Feierstein
—S.C.

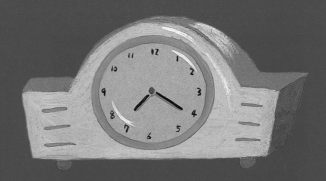

for Noriko
Kimura
—S.Y.

LATE for SCHOOL!

The artist would like to acknowledge the following people:
Yukiko Tomishima, Yumiko Sato, Jess A. Hara, Kim Lampers,
Mikako Sullivan, and Namiko Rudi.

Carolrhoda Books
A division of Lerner Publishing Group, Inc.
241 First Avenue North
Minneapolis, MN 55401 U.S.A.

Website address: www.lernerbooks.com

Library of Congress Cataloging-in-Publication Data

Calmenson, Stephanie.
      Late for school! / by Stephanie Calmenson ; illustrated by Sachiko Yoshikawa.
         p.   cm.
      Summary: When Mr. Bungles the teacher oversleeps, he goes to great lengths,
trying every form of transportation he can find, to get to school on time.
      ISBN: 978-1-57505-935-8 (lib. bdg : alk. paper)
      [1. Tardiness—Fiction. 2. Transportation—Fiction. 3. Stories in rhyme.]
   I. Yoshikawa, Sachiko, ill. II. Title.
   PZ8.3.C13Lat 2008
   [E]—dc22   2007034776

Manufactured in the United States of America
1 2 3 4 5 6 — JR — 13 12 11 10 09 08

LATE for SCHOOL!

Stephanie
Calmenson

illustrations by
Sachiko
Yoshikawa

Carolrhoda Books Minneapolis • New York

You must have forgotten
to set your . . .

clock!

Oh, no!

I'm the teacher
and it's my rule

to never, **ever, ever** be late for . . .

school !

Where is my shoe?

It can't be far.

I'm turning the key.
Oh, what a pain!

My car won't start. I'll race for the . . .

train!

Stop, train, stop!

I can't break my rule
to never, **ever**, **ever** be late for . . .

school!

I missed the train. I won't make a fuss.
Down the street, I can catch the . . .

The people are squeezed
like sardines in a can.

Wait, I'm in luck!
I can hop in this . . .

park!

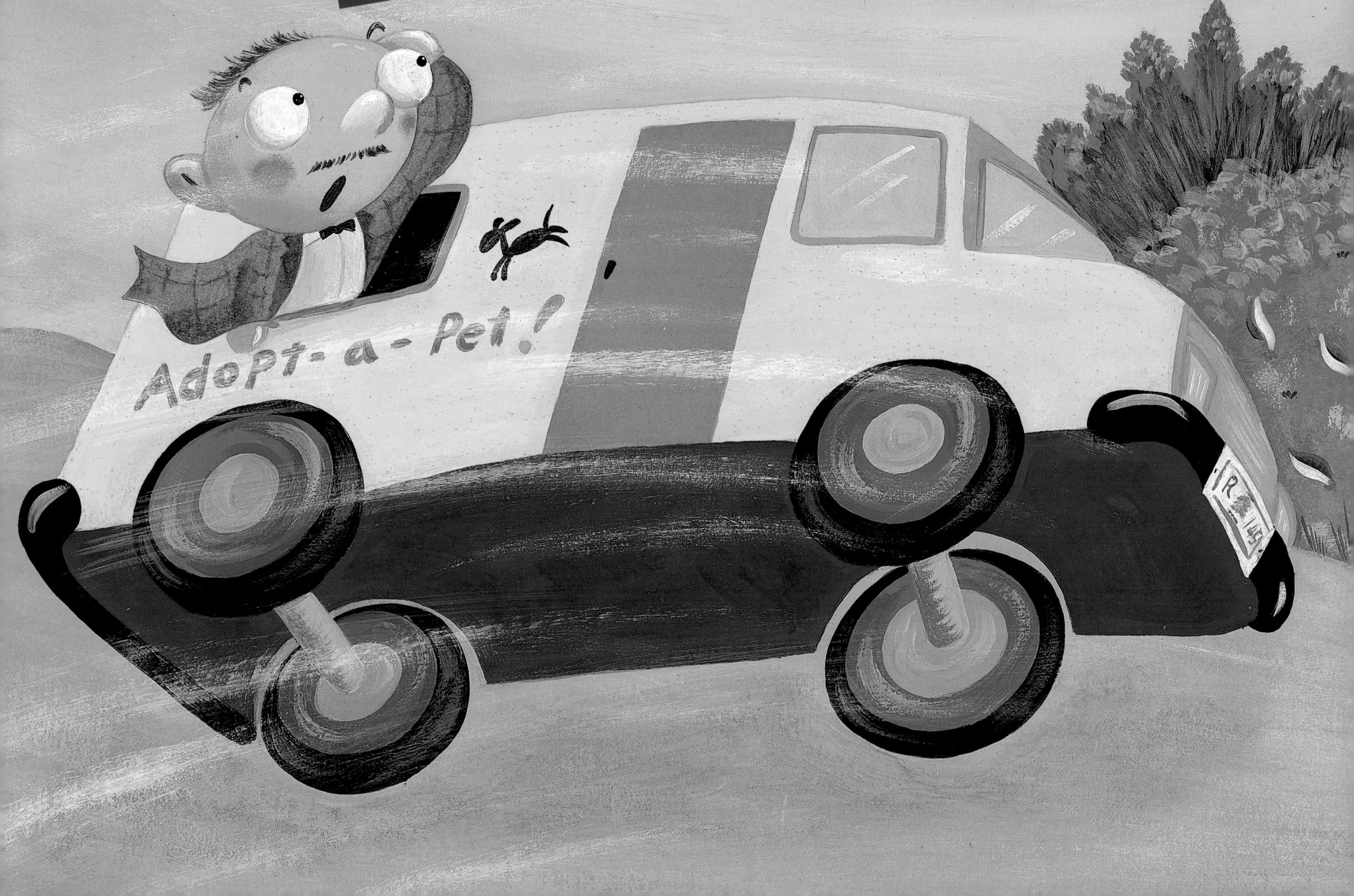

Look what's in the sky!

I can be at school soon
if I catch a ride on that . . .

Stop pecking, birds.
This isn't a meal.
Hiss!

Down

we

go.

Look, there's a . . .

And now it's time to change my . . .

Never, Ever, Ever be late for school!

rule!

Please try your best to be on time for school!!